CONTENTS

From dawn to dusk, the **SCHOOL BUS OF HORRORS** rumbles along city streets and down country roads, searching for another passenger. Yellow, black markings, dirty windows – it looks like any other school bus.

But **BEWARE!** Step aboard this bus and

experience the scariest ride of your life . . .

CHAPTER ONE
HANDS AND ARMS

Iris and her classmates hurry onto a strange school bus. Today they are going on a field trip.

It's easy to find seats. Many children are ill at home.

Some have been off sick for weeks.

"This bus is so old," Iris says.
"And hot!"

"So what," says a boy across the
aisle. "Just open a window."

SWISH! BANG! The bus door closes.

The boy across the aisle opens his window.

Then a voice rumbles through the air. "Keep all hands and arms inside the bus."

The teacher smiles. "You heard the bus driver, children," says Mrs Cogg. "Inside the bus. We all must do our part."

CHAPTER TWO
RING FINGER

Mrs Cogg walks past Iris's seat and then stops.

"What's that on your finger?" the teacher asks Iris.

"Oh, nothing," says Iris.

The boy across the aisle hangs
his arm out of the window.

Mrs Cogg frowns. "Harvey!
What did the driver just say?"
she asks. "Hands inside the bus."

"But it's so hot in here!" Harvey
complains.

When the teacher turns away,
Iris stares at the large purple ring
on her finger.

The ring belongs to Iris's classmate
Serena, who always keeps the ring in
her desk.

But Serena is at home ill today.

Iris plans to put the ring back
in Serena's desk after the field trip.
Then no one will know she took it.

*It looks better on my hand than on
Serena's,* thinks Iris. *Her hands have
too many freckles.*

CHAPTER THREE
UNDERFOOT

SSKKRAAAAAYYP!

A sound makes Iris look up.
The bus is travelling between two
rows of trees.

*Did a branch scrape against the
window?* she wonders.

SSKKRAAAAAYYP!

The sound is coming from below
her feet. A crack in the metal floor
grows wider.

Iris watches as a small object pokes through the crack.

A finger!

Then another finger.

Finally, a hand reaches out from the crack – a hand covered in freckles!

"Ahh!" Iris screams. But at the same time, the driver hits the brakes.

No one hears her.

Mrs Cogg rushes to the front of the bus. "Driver, why did you stop?" she asks.

A low voice rumbles. "The engine. The bus needs more parts."

The hand near Iris's feet has slipped back into the crack.

Iris sees the driver getting up from his seat. He moves like a shadow out of the door.

Mrs Cogg runs after him.
She wants to know what is wrong.

When she leaves, the children cheer. They jump from seat to seat.

UUUNNHHHHH! Iris hears a grunt.

The driver is now standing outside her window.

"More parts," he says through the dirty glass.

CHAPTER FOUR
BODY WORK

Iris stares at the bus driver.
She can't speak.

The driver moves like a smudgy
shadow on the glass.

BANG! BANG!

He is working at the side of the bus, just below her window.

The driver said something was wrong with the engine, thinks Iris. *But the engine is at the front of the bus.*

What is he doing? Iris wonders.

"More parts," comes a voice. "More parts."

The voice sounds like a young girl.

The freckled hand reaches out and grabs Iris by the foot.

"**AAAHH!**" Iris bends down to free her foot.

KRIKK!

Her ring catches on the edge of the crack.

"My hand is stuck!" cries Iris. "Help!"

The girl's voice drifts up from the metal crack. "Yes," it says. "We can always use a hand."

No one is on the bus to hear Iris scream again.

No one sees her get dragged through the crack in the floor.

CHAPTER FIVE
MORE PARTS

Darkness and heat surround Iris.

She smells petrol and burned rubber.

She hears a thudding sound. It shakes through her body.

"You!" says a voice.

Iris sees a girl's face in the dark.
"Serena," she cries.

"I suppose you want your ring back," says Iris.

She twists at the purple ring, but it won't come off her finger.

"Who cares about a ring?" says Serena. "This bus will not move without us."

The darkness grows thick. Iris sees more bodies around them.

She recognizes all of the children from school who have been off sick.

"What are you talking about?" asks Iris.

"The bus," says Serena. "The bus needs a hand."

Serana grabs Iris's hand and pulls her towards a lever.

The sick children are standing by other levers. They move them up and down.

"Keep it moving," they chant. "Keep it moving."

The children crowd around the two girls. "Without us, no bus. Without us, no bus."

"We all must do our part," says Serena.

SCREEEEEEEE-EEEEEEEEEEE!

Mrs Cogg climbs back on to the bus. The children are quiet.

No one notices that Iris is missing.

One of the children, Lacey, jumps into Iris's old seat.

A dark blur moves from the door to the steering wheel.

The bus starts up again.

WHOMP! KLINK! There is a bang and a rattle.

"Now what's wrong?" asks Mrs Cogg.

"More parts again," rumbles the voice from the steering wheel.

"We'll need new parts."

Lacey hears a tiny sound below her.

She sees a hand reaching out
from a crack in the floor.

There is a purple ring on one of
the fingers.

GLOSSARY

aisle path that runs between seats on a bus

complain say you are unhappy about something

lever bar or rod used to run or adjust something

petrol flammable liquid for fuelling engines

rumble make or move with a low, heavy rolling sound

smudgy stained with spots and streaks

DISCUSS

1. Why do you think this book is called *Auto Body Parts*?

2. Do you think other children will join Iris beneath the floor of the bus? Why or why not?

3. What is your favourite illustration in this book? Explain why it's your favourite.

WRITE

1. Create a new title for this book. Then write a paragraph on why you chose your new title.

2. In this book, the bus driver is described as a shadowy blur. Write a story about where the bus driver came from.

3. Write about the scariest bus journey you've ever experienced.